For all the children who can't
hug the ones they love.

P.D. and E.M.

First published in the UK in 2020
First published in the US in 2020
by Faber and Faber Limited
Bloomsbury House, 74–77 Great Russell Street, London WC1B 3DA
Text © Eoin McLaughlin, 2020 Illustrations © Polly Dunbar, 2020 Designed
by Faber and Faber
ISBN 978-0-571-36559-3
Printed in Europe
10 9 8 7 6 5 4 3 2 1
The moral rights of Eoin McLaughlin and Polly Dunbar have been asserted. A
CIP record for this book is available from the British Library.

MIX
Paper from
responsible sources
FSC® C002795

Eoin McLaughlin ♥ Polly Dunbar

While We Can't Hug

faber

Hedgehog and Tortoise were the best of friends.
They wanted to give each other a great, big hug.

But they weren't allowed to touch.

"Don't worry," said Owl.
"There are lots of ways
to show someone you
love them."

Hedgehog tried a wave.

That made Tortoise smile.

Tortoise made a funny face.
That made Hedgehog laugh.

Hedgehog wrote a letter.

And Tortoise wrote one back.

And when Tortoise did a little dance,
Hedgehog joined in, too.

Hedgehog blew a kiss

across the gap

between

them.

Tortoise saw it, and caught it, and kept it.

And sent three back again.

Tortoise sang a song.
Hedgehog played along.

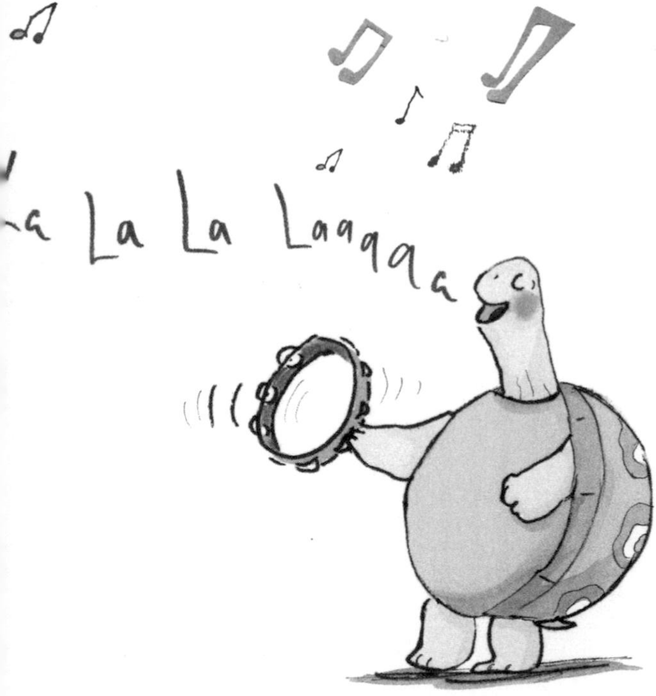
La La Laaaaa

Then they both painted pictures,

so that everyone would know they
were friends . . .

. . . through rain . . .

. . . and shine.

They could not touch.

They could not hug.

But they both knew

that they were loved.